Off to Town!

Written by Hawys Morgan
Illustrated by Maïté Schmitt

Collins

The queen is off to town.

3

The cart turns. Oops!

The queen has weeds in her hair.

Her gown is torn.

A toad is in her boot.

Her maid zooms into sight.

11

The queen feels better.

The pair join in the fun.

To town!

After reading

Letters and Sounds: Phase 3

Word count: 60

Focus phonemes: /ai/ /ee/ /igh/ /oa/ /oo/ /oo/ /ar/ /or/ /ur/ /ow/ /oi/ /air/ /er/

Common exception words: to, the, I, put, into

Curriculum links: Understanding the world

Early learning goals: Reading: read and understand simple sentences; use phonic knowledge to decode regular words and read them aloud accurately; read some common irregular words

Developing fluency

- Your child may enjoy hearing you read the book.
- Discuss with your child how the queen might speak, then take turns to read a page, including any speech bubbles. Demonstrate how the queen's different feelings can be expressed through the tone of her speaking voice.

Phonic practice

- Focus on the /ai/ and /air/ words. Ask your child to read out the following words:

  fair   hair   maid   pair

- Challenge them to read these /ai/ and /air/ words:

  rain   lair   tail   air   pain

Extending vocabulary

- Ask your child to suggest synonyms (words or phrases that have a similar meaning) for these:

  page 2: off (*going*)   page 4: turns (e.g. *leans, topples*)   page 9: not fair (e.g. *unfair, bad luck*)

  page 10: maid (e.g. *servant, helper*)   page 10: zooms into sight (e.g. *appears, runs up*)